A Flavor of Stories

(Short Stories by Paul Jones)

PAUL JONES

Order this book online at www.trafford.com
or email orders@trafford.com

Most Trafford titles are also available at major online book retailers.

Print information available on the last page.

ISBN: 978-1-6987-1078-5 (sc)
ISBN: 978-1-6987-1080-8 (hc)
ISBN: 978-1-6987-1079-2 (e)

Library of Congress Control Number: 2022900343

Trafford rev. 01/12/2022

www.trafford.com

North America & international
toll-free: 844-688-6899 (USA & Canada)
fax: 812 355 4082

Contents

The End of The Rainbow

It was the middle of the summer, but the nights were dark and cold. It stank of blood and guts. "We had been in this God-forsaken place far too long. My men and I were trapped, like some rats in a cat house. When you are hard-pressed, what can one do? Our food was low, and the water, oh, yeah, there was plenty of water, but none to drink because it was filled with corpses and stink!"

"I don't think I can make it!"

"Don't be silly, son, we all are going to make it."

"I know what I told him, but you see, I to had little hope for our survival. Hell, I didn't even know if I wanted to survive. The hurt, the pain, the stink, and the fear were enough to drive anyone mad. Did I say mad? Fear, yes, I was afraid, very afraid! For what, I could not begin to tell you. It was just a deep-down-in-the-gut fear. It was a fear that could not be explained!"

The sun was beginning to rise. "Wait a minute! Those little hills, those hills, they were not hills at all. They were the remains of my men! It became clear that it was the bodies that I feared, not because they were dead, hell no, but because they were my men.

I don't know if you can call them bodies. It was torn flesh and body parts all around. I tried to hold down what little food I had inside, but I could not. I was able to hold it in my mouth and swallow it back down. I am not crazy! Did I say crazy? You see, I could not let my men see me lose it."

Before the sun could finish coming up, you could see the blistering heat from the sand.

"I can't anymore, aaaaah! Hold on, I must hold on! I can't lose it, no, I can't!"

"It all started when we got this new commander. It's not anything worse than having a commander without balls or one that kisses up!"

"You see, we received this mission. I knew then that it was a mission that we could not accomplish. We were set up to fail. We tried to tell our commander, and he agreed with us, but just as soon as some rank would enter the room, he would tuck his tail. My god, man, grow some balls! You lily-livered piece of sh__. Oh, I must get control. In coming! Damn, that one was too close! Why are we still here? Why can't we just leave? Where would we go, and how would we get there? I curse you, Commander!"

Silence fell on deaf ears.

"The day seemed to be flying by. It was about 7:00 a.m. I had such a chill. It had to be 100 degrees."

"My men, I almost forgot about my men. I have to check on them. My men would do anything in the world for me. They would even give their lives for me, my men. I could not ask for better men."

"You take ole Smithy. He's the oldest one out of the bunch. He is married, been married forty years. He has three kids, two girls and a boy."

"Sanchez, my man Sanchez, a hot-blooded fiery young bulk!

He didn't take crap from nobody!"

I remember once we were at this bar when an old friend of mine was greeting me in our own special way. Well, Sanchez thought that the guy was being a butthole. He walked over to him and knocked the living hell out of him. He did this before I could tell him that we were old buddies. You should have seen his face afterward.

"My family, well, you see that I have no one but these guys. I had a wife, but we never had kids. She left me. She said that she wasn't happy. Now she has this guy, and all he ever does is cheat on her, drink, and I heard that he even touches her up, every now and then. I guess she's happy now!"

"Incoming!"

"Wow! That one was too close! My men, where are my men?

They are gone! Why did this have to happen? So many wars, so many deaths."

NURSE: Major, are you telling your war stories again? It's time for your sponge bath and your medication, you know, your little pot of gold.

At the end of the rainbow is a pot of gold.
So, this is the story that I've been told,
I searched over the mountains and over the hills,
But all I ever found is this little cup of pills.

Population Pollution

The night was cold and dark, although it was the middle of summer. There weren't any birds singing nor were there breeze blowing. If it had not been for the calendar, you would not have known what season it was. All life seemed to have left the earth. If it had not been for this one special little creature, the earth would have been void.

They looked down on the earth, and they saw that their work was done. They looked at each other with much pleasure.

"We did the job. Wait, what is this? There is something moving. What could it be? We did enough to destroy all of them! Maybe we did underestimate their kind. Maybe they do have enough will to survive."

"No, it could not be, they were on the verge of destroying themselves, and we just stepped in to speed up the process."

"What do we do now? I know, let us destroy him too."

"No, wait. Let's just watch, he might just destroy himself."

"What if we were wrong? What if they really had what it took to keep their kind going?"

"How can they survive? We have just one left. What can he do?"

"Just trust me, you with so little faith."

"You mean to tell me that we did all this so that we could just let one survive?"

"Calm down, picture it like this: We now have something to play with."

"So you are saying that we can do whatever we want to him?"

"Well, with my authorization only."

"I knew there was going to be a catch to it."

"Hold your tongue. Are you with me or not? I feel that you are not. I tell you what, I'm going to send you down there to keep him company."

"No, I beg of you, please do not send me back, for he will truly kill me!"

"We will see, won't we? All I have to do is to decide on how and when I'll send you back."

"Do you think it is wise for you to send her back?"

"Oh, you question me too!"

"No, I do not question your decision, but with her knowing all that she knows . . ."

"Yes, I can see where that might develop into a problem. From this point, she will not remember any of this nor will she remember any of us. Send her!"

"Now that we have two of them down there, what shall we call them?"

"I have the perfect names, Abraham and Elaine!"

"I must introduce them in a manner that it would be natural to them. I'll wait until he goes to sleep, and when he wakes, he will see her."

"Okay. What about her? How will she come to know him?"

"Yes, once again, you are right, and once again, I have the answer. She will just see him. Don't forget that she has no memory."

So it was done. The male creature, Abe, falls into a deep sleep.

The female was placed by his side. When Abe opened his eyes, he was excited, and yet he was afraid. He wanted to touch the beautiful dark-skinned creature, but he didn't know how to go about doing so.

"I told you that it was no use to save him. We should have destroyed him, along with the rest of his kind."

"Hold it down and just watch. We must give it some time. Besides, it's still not too late. We can always destroy them whenever we want."

Abe looked once again at her ravishing dark skin, and he wanted so bad to touch her, not in a lustful way, but to embrace her, to feel and care for her and to show compassion for one of his own.

Abe finally decided to touch her, but he knew to touch her on the shoulder.

He touched her and shaking her oh so gently.

ABE: Are you okay? Are you hurt? Are you alive?

Abe got no response, but he could see her exquisite breast rise and fall, so he knew that she, indeed, was alive. He dared not to touch her again, but he could not help but wonder what she would feel like pressed against his body. Instead, he went and sat, just keeping an eye on her while keeping her safe. Abe felt so excited that he was not the only one of his kind left.

Elaine moved. Abe stood up. He wanted to present himself as an upright creature, someone to be proud of. It was a bit premature. You see, she did not wake up. She only turned over.

Abe walked away.

"You see, I told you that they were not worth saving. He has not the patience to wait. He would just leave his own kind, and for what? Can he not see there's not any more of his kind around? So where is he going? Why is he leaving?"

"My, talking about who has no patience. If you would just sit and watch, I'm sure that all your questions will be answered."

It seemed as if hours had passed, but it had only been a few minutes.

"He has not returned yet, let both of them die."

"You are getting beside yourself. I'm still in charge, and I alone decide when and if they die!"

"Well, shall we wake her?"

"No, I want our male subject to be here when she wakes."

"I really don't see the point in wanting him to be there when she wakes. If he returns and she is awake, we can still see his reaction."

"You do have a point. I will wake her and let her roam. Plus, it will give us a chance to see her reactions as well."

He reached down and touched her so gently. She looked around.

She thought that she heard a noise. It was not. It was just the cool breeze blowing by. She started walking away, but she knew not where to go, so she just sat down where she was and started looking around.

"I will put him on the path so that they may meet, then we will decide what to do from that point."

Abe saw Elaine, and he was delighted to meet her, but she was afraid. She wanted to turn and run, but where? So she hid behind a rock. It was the only place she could find to hide. Abe tried to reach out for her, but she was still afraid. He finally got close enough to touch her, and when he did, she knew from that moment that he would be there for her.

"What are you trying to do? I thought you were trying to destroy them and not replenish it!"

"Watch your tone!"

Abe and Elaine liked each other very much, and shortly afterward, they started to multiply, and there were little ants all over the place.

We are tiny little creatures, but we are strong.
We will be here even when you're gone.
You step on us, and our spirit, you try to crush,
But the words that I've spoken, you can surely trust.

A Cry for Help

We open up with two young girls in senior high school; one is from a fairly wealthy family, and the other, well, let's just say that she would be labeled as a have-not.

JILL: Girl, I would do anything to live your life.

ONIKA: You must be out your mind! You got a momma and daddy at the house, no sisters or brothers, you wear name-brand clothes, you have the top-of-the-line phone, and you drive a brand-new Camaro SS. Girl, you must be out your mind! What? What type of grades you got, all As, huh? I'll change with you any old day. I have three brothers and two sisters that I have to share not only one bedroom with, but one bed with also. Huh, I even have to ride the bus.

JILL: Yeah, it does appear like I have it going on, huh? Yeah, I got a mom and a dad at home, but my dad is out every other night, trying to screw everything he can put his little man in, and my mom sits at the house trying to drink herself to death. No sisters or brothers, huh? I wish I had a sister or a brother, someone I could turn to or just talk to. They buy me name-brand clothes and nice things so they won't have to spend time with me or talk to me.

My grades, I do my best just to try to impress them so that maybe one day they will notice me, but it doesn't work.

ONIKA: Girl, I didn't know. I thought you had it going on.

JILL: I wish sometimes that I was never born. It is so hard going home every evening not knowing if I'm going to find my mother lying on the bathroom floor, in her own vomit, or with her head in the toilet and then hearing my dad come home late lying, saying that he was working, cursing my mom, with both of them screaming, how much they hate each other. Yeah, I got it good.

ONIKA: What? Am I supposed to feel sorry for you? If you are so tired of it, why don't you leave or something?

What Onika didn't know was that Jill had just left a note to her mom and dad, telling them that she could not take it anymore, that she was never coming home again, and that they didn't have to look for her because they would know exactly where to find her, that they shouldn't cry because they didn't have the right to.

The rest of the day, while at school, Jill was being overly generous. She gave away several personal items to some friends and others. Before the end of the day, she made her rounds telling all her teachers that it was a pleasure knowing them and that she would truly miss them. At the beginning of sixth period, she took three Xanax bars.

The final bell sounded, ending the day. Jill staggered out to her vehicle, got in, started it up, and slowly drove toward the parking lot exit. She headed east on the highway until she got to the expressway. She then turned north on to the southbound Lane. High on Xanax and not thinking clearly, she pushed the accelerator to the floor, 60,

70, 80, 90, up to 120 miles per hour. The gap between her and an eighteen-wheeler semi-truck closed quickly. She and the truck hit head on. Her vehicle appeared to just break apart as she flew out of the front window, shredded like ground beef.

Meanwhile, at Jill's house, her mother had just finished off a fifth of gin and was about to open up another when she turned on the news.

REPORTER: I'm at the scene of this fatal accident involving an eighteen-wheeler and a black Camaro SS. Names have not been released pending the notification of kin. Witnesses state that the Camaro was traveling at a very high rate of speed, and it's apparent that the driver of this car was on the wrong side of the expressway. Speaking with law enforcement, they stated that there were not any skid marks, meaning that the car either didn't see the semi or the driver intentionally ran headfirst into it. I'm Max Jones reporting from this tragic accident for channel 7 news.

Jill's mother had a sinking feeling in the pit of her stomach.

All of a sudden, the doorbell rang, *ding-dong. Knock, knock, knock.* She didn't have to ask. She knew who it was and what they were there for. As she opened the door, she dropped the bottle of gin.

It shattered on the floor. It was a police officer; he came in and introduced himself.

JILL'S MOTHER: Tell me, tell me, no, don't tell me, my baby, she's dead, isn't she?!

She took off running. She ran to Jill's room with the officer behind her. She opened the door and looked around the room, and on the dresser was a note from Jill.

JILL'S MOTHER: Read it! Can you please read it?!

OFFICER JORDAN: Dear parents, by the time you get this letter, I will be gone, never to come here anymore. I want to say that I am truly sorry for ever being born. I am sorry that you two felt that you had to stay together just for my sake. I am sorry, Mother, that I caused you to turn into a lush and you, Dad, into a whore! It was not my plan to be such a burden to you, but as of today, I will not burden you anymore. You will not have to look for me because by this time, you probably know where I am. I want to end this note by telling you two that I do love you very much, but to be perfectly honest with you, I don't know what love is because you never showed me.

JILL'S MOTHER: My baby! It's my fault!

She ran toward Officer Jordan. He put his arms out, and she ran into them, crying. He then escorted her back to the front room. Just as soon as they reach the front room, Jill's father entered.

He didn't have to ask what was going on because he had already heard. Officer Jordan handed him the note. He began reading it, but halfway through, he went down on his knees, covering his head with both hands while tears streamed down his face.

After the funeral, wanting to be alone, the mother went back to the house and found all her bottles of gin and any other type of liquor and poured them out. She then began to clean the house, and after she had cleaned the house, she then began fixing herself. She went into the bathroom, the one where she had spent many nights on the floor, and took a warm shower, then she got out and fixed her hair and her makeup. She put on a lovely blue dress and heels, and then with tears still in her eyes, she simply just sat down.

Dad left the funeral and went on to do what he loved doing the most. But this time there was something different. Being out with one of his mistresses wasn't the same. It just felt different. He was lying in bed with her head on his chest when, suddenly, he tossed her off him. He tossed her onto the floor.

DAD: I can't do this anymore. I just can't. I killed my daughter because of you and other women like you. I killed my daughter!

I destroyed my family being with women like you! I've got to get out of here. I've got to go!

Walking toward his ZR1, he started thinking. He really didn't know where he was going. He started toward home, but he thought, *Is it still my home? Does she blame me? Can I live with myself?* He had so many questions and too few answers.

He made it to his house, he put the key in the lock, he opened the door, and when he walked in, he saw his wife, the woman he married over twenty years ago. She was as beautiful as the first day they met.

DAD: I am so sorry, so, so sorry. I haven't been the man I should have been. I wasn't the father. I am so sorry!

She stood up and walked toward him. She put a finger up to his mouth, indicating for him not to say a word.

MOTHER, sobbing: We are both to blame. We just got caught up in our lives and never made time for the most important thing in our lives, and now she's gone.

DAD: Where do we go from here?

They looked at each other with blanks stares on their faces, not knowing what was going to be next.

DAD: Lord, help us!

We have been blessed with so much stuff
But for some reason, we forgot about us.
With whom are we to be mad
Because we lost the love that we once had?
Don't get caught up in money and things
And the false happiness that it seems to bring.

Making A Decision

SHOULD I DO IT?

Standing in their spacious family room, a father and son are in deep conversation.

LARRY: Dad, I want a new car.

DAD: You want a what, a new car? Tell me, why am I supposed to buy a new car?!

LARRY: I'm your son, for one, and I do have a job.

DAD: What about me having to come to the school four out of five days? How about you being suspended from school? And how about you failing all your classes?! Son, I wouldn't feel comfortable investing in a car for you . . .

LARRY: That's fine, you don't have to agree to buy me one.

DAD: Hold on, don't you dare interrupt me! And you better not ask your mother! As a matter of fact, the only reason I let you drive at all is because you do have a job, but you have just messed that up. From this moment on, either your mother or I will take you and pick you up from work. Got that? Give me my key! Now go and clean that nasty room of yours!

Larry's dad knew that if he asked his mother, she would continue to bug him. But this was one thing that he was determined to not give in to. They were not going to buy Larry a new car.

Larry walked off to his room, wanted to slam the door, but thought it would be better not to. Instead of cleaning his room, he picked up his phone and called one of his homeboys.

LARRY: Hey, Chris, man, what's up? You can't imagine what just happened to me. My punk-a— dad just told me that he was not going to buy me a new car, and he took the keys to the old rust bucket that I was driving. He said that he or my mom would take me and pick me up from work.

CHRIS: Damn, man, that is lame, so whatcha gonna do?

LARRY: I don't know yet. Hell, it's not like he doesn't have the money. I know that. Hell, he got bank! It got to be a way for me to get one!

CHRIS: Why did he say he wasn't gonna get you one?

LARRY: Get this, his punk a— talking about my school stuff, about me getting suspended and my grades. Hell, I don't need the school anyway. I got a job now. Man, let me hit you back.

This chicken head Kay is calling.

CHRIS: I thought that you didn't like her?

LARRY: I don't, but she got some fire head!

CHRIS: Yeah, bet?

LARRY: Hey, girl, I was just thinking about you.

KAY: As you can tell, I was thinking about you too. Why don't you come over? I'm hungry.

LARRY: Damn, girl, as good as that sounds, you hungry, huh?

I can't. My sorry-a— dad took the keys to the rust bucket from me.

KAY: You shouldn't talk like that about your parents. They take very good care of you, and they basically get you anything you want.

LARRY: Yeah, well, why the hell can't I get a new car? I wish his punk a— was dead! Then I know that I could get all that I wanted.

KAY: You shouldn't say things like that.

LARRY: I mean it, I wish he was dead! I'm gone. I will talk with you later. And by the way, stay hungry!

KAY: Always for you.

Larry hangs up and then calls Chris back.

LARRY: Hey, dude, I'm back. Man, that chicken head talking about she was hungry, you know what she wants, and I don't have time for her.

CHRIS: Hey, me and some fellows getting ready to hit the mall, you want to come?

LARRY: What, you coming to pick me up?

CHRIS: Hell yeah!

LARRY: Come on, but park a little down the street. I will meet you.

After Larry got off the phone, he picked up his clothes from on top of his bed and threw them underneath his bed, and all his stuff that were on top of his dresser, he racked it into his top dresser drawer. After he finished, he started looking out of his window. He saw Chris, Sam, and Jerome pull up in Chris's new black Charger.

He jumped out of his window, ran to the corner, and jumped in. "Homeboy, homeboy."

SAM: Let's ride, let's go get some guts. Hey, you got some money? What about us going to get some smokes?

CHRIS: Sounds good to me!

SAM: Hell yeah!

LARRY: What about you, Jerome?

JEROME: You know that I don't smoke, but if that's what you all want to do, so be it, but don't count me in on it.

CHRIS: Leave him alone, Larry, Jerome's cool.

The only place that they could get some smokes (marijuana) was on the other side of town. That side was known for its dope dealers, prostitutes, and crack heads. As they turned the corner, a dirty old dude walked up to the passenger's side.

BUM: Hey, fellows, I do all of y'all for twenty.

LARRY: Drive, Chris, drive.

Chris drove off.

SAM: Larry, man, Chris was telling me about your little problem.

LARRY: Chris, man!

SAM: Yo, man, it's cool. Your old man got life insurance? Hell, I know how you can get that new car plus.

They pulled up to this little old lady sitting on her front porch.

OLD LADY: How may I help you, boys?

SAM: We need some smoke!

OLD LADY: How deep is your pockets?

SAM: Twenty deep.

OLD LADY: Wait here.

The old lady turned around and went into the house. She soon returned with a balled-up plastic bag.

OLD LADY: Show me your green, and I will give you some green.

Sam was the only one braved enough to hold the money, so he showed the old lady two $10 bills, and they made the exchange.

SAM: Hell yeah, let roll a fat one.

You could tell that the rest of the boys were not as anxious as Sam was to smoke, but they went along, all but Jerome. He was the only one who stood his ground.

LARRY: Sam, man, you were saying something about getting my new car.

SAM: Pass the blunt, man. And I said something to the fact of you getting anything you want, not just a new car.

LARRY: Well, how can I do that?

SAM: You must be willing to take a chance to make a decision.

LARRY: Chance, decision, what are you talking about?

SAM: Smoke this one up and fire up another one, and I will tell you.

Sam and Larry smoked the entire first one before they realized that Chris didn't hit it at all.

SAM: Damn, Chris, man, you gonna hit any of this?

LARRY: Look, Sam, are you going to tell me what you were talking about or not?

SAM: Look, man, you said that you can get anything from your momma, right?

LARRY: Yeah, so what's that got to do with anything? If my dad tells my mom that I can't have something, then she will side with him.

SAM: What if your dad wasn't around anymore? Here, take a couple more hits.

Larry took a few more hits as he thought of what Sam was trying to say.

CHRIS: Sam, what in the hell are you trying to say? No, don't tell me because I don't want to be a witness to anything. As a matter of fact, when we get to the mall, you two make sure you go in a different direction from me and Jerome.

SAM: Chris, man, stop being such a pussy. First, you don't want to hit the smokes, and now you and your punk-a— brother is acting like a little bi—h.

CHRIS: Sam, you can talk about me, but leave my brother out of this! Keep talking, and you and Larry can get out now.

SAM: All right, Chris, man, it's cool. I will wait to talk with Larry when we are alone.

Chris continued to drive, never taking a hit of the weed. They soon made it to the mall.

CHRIS: Hey, Sam, why don't you and Larry just get out here and Jerome and I will come in after I park?

SAM: All right, man, but, Chris, don't leave us, man.

CHRIS: I'm not that low down. I said that we were coming in, and we are, and besides, this will give you and Larry time to talk.

Larry and Sam got out of the car and started walking toward the mall.

LARRY: What's up, man?

SAM: Look, man, all I'm saying is that if your ole man wasn't around, you could probably talk your mom into anything, right?

LARRY: Yeah, you're right. But where is my dad going?

SAM: Fool, don't be so stupid! We get rid of his punk a—.

Larry started thinking.

LARRY: Get rid of him, how? Are you talking about killing him?

SAM: What the hell you think I've been talking about?

LARRY: Man, I'm high, but I'm not stupid!

SAM: So you gonna be a punk all your life? You even said that if he wasn't around, you could get whatever you wanted from your mother!

LARRY: Yeah, but I wouldn't dare think about killing my own dad.

SAM: You don't have to do it yourself. You can get someone else to do it.

LARRY: Let me think about it.

Larry walked away from Sam, thinking that he had completely lost his mind. There was no way he would ever consider killing his father. After all, he still loved him, and he had always been there for him. Larry right then thought that he would talk to Sam and tell him that if he ever mentioned the thought of killing his dad again, that it wouldn't be his dad who would die.

LARRY: Sam, you must be out of your mind. There is no way I would ever consider killing my dad, and if you ever mention it again, it will not be him dying!

SAM: Calm down, man, that's what I wanted to hear. I wanted you to realize how much you really cared about your dad and how much he really loves you. He has been there for you all the way. He has given you everything. I wish I had a dad like yours. As a matter of fact, I wish I had a dad. My dad denied that I was his child and went on to have another family. Man, appreciate what you have.

LARRY: I see what you're talking about. I guess I should go home and talk to him, huh?

SAM: Yeah, how about us throwing away this bag of weed and waiting until your high wears off?

LARRY: I never really thought you would be the one to make me understand. Yeah, my girl tried telling me the same thing, but I wouldn't listen. Man, it cost me $10 to learn what I already had. Man, I appreciate you.

SAM: Man, just think about it, it only cost you $20 to help you realize that you have one hell of a dad.

LARRY: Twenty? I paid in ten.

SAM: Uh, you're going to give my ten back. That's my fee for the advice. That makes it even better. Now let's wait for those two and see what we can see and then get up out of here. Oh yeah, you probably need to call Kay back also.

LARRY: Yeah, once again, you're right. I do need to call Kay back, and I probably need to start treating her better. After all, she is someone's daughter, and I guess I really do like her, and I know that she likes me, but first, I need to talk to my dad. I think I'll tell him that he doesn't have to worry about coming to the school again and I'm going to do my best from here on out.

SAM: Now you're talking.

Learn to appreciate your mom and dad.
It doesn't matter if their decisions make you
happy or mad. They are there to look
out for you. The love they have for you
is simple and true.

Mr. Wind

We open with one of the most powerful and the most mysterious elements ever known.

Mr. Wind was bored one day, so he decided to go and see what he could get into. So he blew over to Mr. Ocean's.

Mr. Ocean was lying there, minding his own business, and all of a sudden, he was startled.

MR. OCEAN: Well, hello. Who are you? Where did you come from?

MR. WIND: Oh, I'm Mr. Wind.

MR. OCEAN: Okay, I'm Mr. Ocean, but my friends call me Water. What do you do, Mr. Wind?

MR. WIND: Well, I just go here and there, moving things.

MR. OCEAN: Moving things, moving things like what?

MR. WIND: Anything that I set my mind to move, I just move it.

As a matter of fact, I bet I can move you.

MR. OCEAN: Move me? What makes you think that I want to be moved? And besides, what makes you think that you can move me?

MR. WIND: I knew you would say that. That's what they all say just before I move them. I tell you what, once I prove that I can move you, you will have to go on and off the shore at certain times of the day.

MR. OCEAN: And if you can't?

MR. WIND: If I can't, I will just blow away, and I will never bother you again.

MR. OCEAN: Okay, have at it, move me! Because right now, you're starting to annoy me.

Mr. Wind started to swell and swell. He started blowing so hard that Mr. Ocean started to move back and forth.

MR. OCEAN: Okay, okay, you've proved your point. I can't believe that someone as light as you could move me. I will hold up to my end of the bargain. I will have a high tide and a low tide, if that's okay with you?

MR. WIND: I knew you would see it my way. I'll see you later.

Mr. Wind moved on until he came across this beautiful white sand. He thought, *I bet I can make her move. She's just sitting there all relaxed. Let me make a bet with her as well.*

MR. WIND: Well, hello there, you look mighty fine just resting there.

MRS. SANDS: Oh, hello there, you startled me. I didn't see you. Well, I still don't see you. I guess I should have said that I didn't hear you.

MR. WIND: Hello, I'm Mr. Wind.

MRS. SANDS: Well, hello, Mr. Wind, and thank you. I'm Mrs. Sands, but my friends call me Sandy.

MR. WIND: Okay, Sandy, what is it that you do?

SANDY: I just lie around all day, and people come around and play with me. They dig me up, and they have a wonderful time with me. And you, what is it that you do?

MR. WIND: Oh, I just go from here and there, moving things.

SANDY: Moving things? What do you want to move things for?

MR. WIND: Well, sometimes you just want to mix things up. Just like you, I bet I can make you move and mix you up.

MRS. SANDS: Well, Mr. Wind, I don't think so. I'm not going anywhere, so I don't think you can move me, and you will just be wasting your time. The people come and go. They move me around, but I just fall right back in place, so like I said, I'm not going anywhere!

MR. WIND: I tell you what, if I move you where you can't fall back in place, every time I come around, you will go wherever I want you to go.

MRS. SANDS: You have a deal. Do your best. Wait a minute. What do I get if you can't move me?

MR. WIND: I tell you what, if I can't move you, I will just blow away and never bother you again.

MRS. SANDS: That sounds good to me because I'm tired of you already! You're beginning to sound like an old windbag.

Mrs. Sands burst out laughing, but Mr. Wind didn't find it too funny.

Mr. Wind started to swell and swell. He started to blow, and Mrs. Sands couldn't stay put. She started to lose grain after grain.

MRS. SANDS: Okay, okay, you've moved me. I will move whenever and wherever you want me to.

Mr. Wind just smiled and decided to move on. And while he was leaving, he came upon a tree.

MR. WIND: Oh hello. How are you? My name is Mr. Wind.

MR. TREE: Hello, my name is Mr. Tree, and that's what my friends call me.

Mr. Tree was usually the strong silent type that didn't like to be bothered.

Mr. Wind saw that Mr. Tree was kind of stuck on himself, so he thought that he would have some fun with him.

MR. WIND: I see you have some lovely limbs.

MR. TREE: Yes, I do, don't I? Mr. Wind, is it? What do you do, and what is it that you want from me?

MR. WIND: Oh, I was just admiring you. You look so elegant, the way you just stand there big and tall, all strong and everything.

MR. TREE: Yes, I try.

MR. WIND: Do you ever move or anything?

MR. TREE: Me, move? Never! I am planted firm, and nothing can move me. My roots run deep! I don't even move from side to side. I'm solid!

MR. WIND: Nothing can move you, huh?

MR. TREE: You heard what I said, nothing!

MR. WIND: What if I told you that I knew something that could move you?

MR. TREE: If something was to move me, then I would sway back and forth, and let it be known that it was more powerful than I. So what is it that you think can move me?

MR. WIND: Me.

Mr. Tree started to laugh.

MR. TREE: You? You who have no substance. You're but just air, hot air at that. How can you move me?

Mr. Wind didn't say another word. He just began to swell and swell, and then he blew harder than he has ever blown before. At first, it looked like Mr. Tree was right. He stood firm. But then all of a sudden, he began to move. He started to move from side to side.

MR. TREE: Okay, stop! You've proved your point. I wouldn't have thought that a weightless substance like you could move me.

But you did, and I will stand by my word. Whenever you come around and you want me to sway, I will.

MR. WIND: Mr. Tree, don't you never underestimate the power of the wind.

Mr. Wind decided to retire for the day, so he just blew away.

Never underestimate the things that you can't see.
You never know the powers that could be.

The Little Lion Princess

In the heart of Africa, we find a very healthy pride of lions.

There was the king, Louie; his bride queen, Lalita; her sisters; and a few younger males.

King Louie and Queen Lalita were expecting, and the day came when the queen had her cubs. She had three cubs. There were Lil Mo, Lil Juan, and the only female out of the litter, Princess Badu.

The lion cubs grew quickly, they played together, but King Louie noticed that Princess Badu was rather aggressive. She was the first to eat, and often she ruled over her brothers.

King Louie decided to speak with the queen to take care of things.

KING LOUIE: Queen Lalita, now you do remember that we males are king the jungle?

She didn't say a word. She just stood there and looked at him.

QUEEN LALITA: What are you trying to say?

KING LOUIE: I see our little princess, Badu, eating first and leading Lil Mo and Lil Juan around, and I repeat, she's eating first!

I suggest that you put her in her place and let her know her position.

Once again, the queen didn't say a word. She didn't like how and what the king was saying, but she still decided to speak to Badu.

QUEEN LALITA: I see that you mentioned that she was eating first twice. That's important to you, huh?

★★★

QUEEN LALITA: Badu, come over here, my child.

She sat her down and licked her head to let her know that she loved her very much, and then she began to speak with her.

QUEEN LALITA: I see that you're always eating before your brothers and that you're always leading them around.

Princess Badu put a smile on her face. She thought that her mother was about to compliment her.

QUEEN LALITA: Well, Badu, we are lioness, and we are to follow the males.

Badu looked confused. She thought that she was doing the right thing. She wanted to be strong. She wanted to take after her dad and be leader.

PRINCESS BADU: But, Momma, I see you and all my aunts killing all our meals, and I see Daddy and the other males push you all to the side and take most of the food. That's not right. Plus, I'm the daughter of the king of the jungle and the queen of the pride!

The queen then looked at Badu, and she then held her head down toward the ground.

QUEEN LALITA: Badu, it's the law of the jungle, and besides, it has always been like this. You see, your daddy protects us, and we hunt for him.

PRINCESS BADU: Momma, just because something has always been done doesn't make it right. And besides, how come Daddy has to protect us? I saw you and my aunts fight off others before. And Daddy is gone all the time. I know what I'm going to do when I grow up. I'm going to start my own pride.

QUEEN LALITA: Now, Badu, just how are you going to do that?

PRINCESS BADU: I'll take all my cousins that want to go with me, and we will start our own pride.

QUEEN LALITA: So just you and your cousins, well, who will protect you all?

PRINCESS BADU: We will gather together, and we will hunt, and we will fight.

QUEEN LALITA: My little princess, what will happen when you grow old? Will your pride just die out?

PRINCESS BADU: Well, Mom what do you want me to do, just bow down and be like the rest of—?

QUEEN LALITA: Watch it, Badu, you're about to overstep your grounds. Baby, first, you must learn who you are, and once you learn that, you will know that it doesn't matter what others think or say. You are the princess, and one day you will be the queen, and you will be the most powerful lioness in the pride. You will have to make decisions for the whole pride. You will have to make sure that the pride has enough to eat, and yes, one day you will have cubs of your own.

PRINCESS BADU: Momma, I didn't mean to make you angry.

QUEEN LALITA: Oh, Badu, my baby, I'm not angry. I'm really glad that we had this talk because you need to know who you are and who you will become. And now it's time for the lionesses and I to go on a hunt.

Just as soon as Queen Lalita said that . . .

KING LOUIE: Lalita, I'm hungry. Have you and the lionesses hunted today?

QUEEN LALITA: Right on time.

Queen Lalita called the other lionesses together.

QUEEN LALITA: Okay, ladies, it's time for us to go and get our meal.

KING LOUIE: Uh, Lalita, did you have that talk with Badu?

QUEEN LALITA: Yes, I did, and I think you might have to accept her for who she is. She will be a great leader one day, and she will still be your daughter. Okay, ladies, let's get dinner.

The queen and the other lionesses went out and saw some wildebeests. The queen set the perimeter, and she told her sisters when to start the chase.

It wasn't long before they had dinner on the ground. The lionesses started to eat, but when they heard King Louie running toward the meal, they backed away. But then Princess Badu ran up and sat beside her father and started to eat. King Louie didn't know what to think. He never had anyone brave enough to sit beside him and eat with him. Queen Lalita was afraid. She didn't know how he would react. She thought maybe he might hurt the princess. The king just looked at her, and then he looked at the queen, as if he was giving his approval.

After dinner, and after all had eaten, the king and queen went to their shady spot.

KING LOUIE: You know what, that little princess will be one of the best leaders this pride has ever had.

QUEEN LALITA: Yes, I know.

They settled down for their midday sleep.

Sometimes you have to break status quo
to follow your heart that no one else can possibly know.

The Country Bumkins

On a hot humid summer day. Deep, deep, deep down in the country, we find two close friends. Their hair was nappy. They had on old T-shirts, some pairs of too-short coveralls, and no shoes. They went by initials DI and PJ. They love going fishing and just hanging out together until one day they saw this girl.

DI: PJ, did you see that there gal?

PJ: Yeah, I seen her. She shows is pretty.

DI: I see her first!

PJ: So what? What that pose to mean?

DI: That mean I get a chance to talk to her first.

PJ: I bet you ain't even goanna get her name.

DI: How's much you wanna bet?

PJ: I got this nickel.

DI: A whole nickel. Now you know you ain't got money. I tell you what, if you catch a fish then I can have it, if I get her name first.

So the two buddies walk off together, trying to catch up with the young girl.

DI: Hey, gal, what your name is?

PJ: Boy, you so stupid! How you gonna get a gal name by just yelling at her?

The young girl turned around. She looked at both of them and turned back around and continued walking.

DI: Hey gal I is talking to you.

PJ: Hey DI just leave her be. She ain't gonna give us her name, and besides, we don't know if she got some big brothers.

The young girl continued to walk as a matter of fact she sped up.

PJ: Look DI she is walking faster. We best to leaving her be.

DI: You just want me to owe you a fish.

PJ: Naw, man, we just best to be leaving her be. Look, you can have the fish. I's got a bad feeling about this gal.

DI: Man shut up; you always got a bad feeling!

PJ: I's telling you we, just might needs, to turn around and goes back a fishing!

All of a sudden, the young girl started to slow down.

DI: Look man she is slowing down! I told you she is gonna give me her name.

PJ: Uh, DI, man I thank we best be turning around and turning around mighty fast. Look!

The young girl had made it to four large males, and she started talking to them and pointing in the direction of DI and PJ.

DI: So what that pose to mean? I ain't afraid of those sap suckers.

PJ: Look, man, you ain't got to be afraid, but I thank common sense tells us that we got a go. They're heading our way!

DI: Look, PJ, you is bigger than me, so you take three, and I takes that small one.

PJ: Man, how comes you is always getting me into these thangs? You, big dummy!

The four rather large boys caught up with DI and PJ. DI hit the smaller boy. But what DI didn't know was that the smaller boy was the strongest, fastest, and the hardest-hitting one out of the four. While PJ was just wrestling with the other three, DI was getting his head beat in.

DI: PJ, help me, man!

PJ ran over to help DI, but then the little guy turned and punched PJ in his nose, and it felt like he had broken it. PJ looked at DI and grabbed him, and they both ran away.

DI: PJ, do I still get to keep the fish?

PJ: Man, I should bust your nose! Naw, you ain't getting no fish, and you owe me a fish, and I's get to pick the one I want. I wonder who them boys was.

DI: I's don't rightly now, but that little one show can hit. He got your nose just a bleeding, just hold your head back.

PJ: Don't touch me, man!

DI and PJ finally made it back to their fishing hole.

DI: She show was pretty!

PJ: Man, just fish. I ain't got no time to be chasing behind no more skirts.

DI: But, PJ . . .

PJ: But my butt! I's finally got the bleeding stop, and I ain't gonna—hold on, just one dab, burn minute!

DI: What?

PJ: You didn't see that fine thang walk over yonder?

DI: Naw, we is here to fish, not to be chasing no skirts.

PJ: Boy, if you don't hush your mouth, I's gonna—hey, come on!

DI and PJ were off again.

DI: I bet you can't even get her name.

PJ: Bet!

DI: I bet you two fishes.

PJ: You ain't even catch one yet.

DI and PJ began to walk behind the young girl.

PJ: Hey, hey, you. I's talking to you.

The young girl turned around. She looked at the both of them and turned back around and started walking faster. DI and PJ stopped and looked at each.

DI: PJ?

PJ: I'm with you.

They turned around and went back to their fishing hole.

PJ: I likes fishing better anyhow.

The Country Bumkins Go to The Store

The two country bumkins were sitting on the front porch of a house. The house was one where you could throw a rock in the front door and it would go out of the back door. They were playing in the dirt, making little pictures with some sticks that they had picked up.

DI: PJ, I's tired of just sitting here.

PJ: What you want a do?

DI: Hey, I's gots a nickel.

PJ: And so?

DI: We can goes to the store.

PJ: I's don't know, every time I's go somewhere with you, some thang happen.

DI: Man, to be so big, you show is scary, for a big guy that is.

PJ: Last time you done near got my nose broke, it still hurts.

DI: Man, come on!

PJ: Okay, but . . .

DI: Man, just comes on!

They started to the store, but as they made it to the block, a young girl approached them.

YOUNG GIRL: Hey, what y'all names?

PJ looked at DI.

PJ: Man, don't do it.

DI stood there with his bare feet, and with his big toe, he started to draw circles in the dirt. PJ started to look around. He was thinking that some big boys might come from around the corner.

DI: My name is DI.

YOUNG GIRL: My name is Pearl. What are you two 'bout to do?

DI: I's going to the stoe.

PEARL: To the store? You have some money?

PJ: Naw, we ain't got no money. We just going to look.

DI: I too got some money. I's got this whole nickel.

PJ just turned around and slapped his forehead.

PJ: DI, don'ts you thank we needs to be going?

DI: Man, don't you see I is busy?

PEARL. What your friend's name?

DI: Aw, that there is PJ. He was about to leave.

PJ: Huh? You done.

DI: Man!

PEARL: He don't have to leave.

DI: You wants to walks with me to the store?

PEARL: I don't have any money.

DI: You ain't got to have no money, you with DI.

PJ: And PJ.

DI: Yeah, yeah.

But before they made it to the next block, this group of guys appeared.

BIG BOY: Hey, what you doing walking with my gal?

PJ started whispering underneath his breath.

PJ: I told you, I told you. You big dummy!

DI: Huh? We was just walking, and she—

PJ: Oh, it we now, huh?

BIG BOY: I's thank you is trying to take my gal.

PEARL: Now, Bubba, he was just takin' me to the store to buys me some candy.

BUBBA: Which one?

DI quickly looked at PJ. And before he knew it, Bubba had hit PJ in the nose. DI grabbed PJ's hand, and they started running. They ran back to the front porch.

PJ: What done happen, man?

DI: What you mean?

PJ: Oh, I's 'member now. I told you, I told you! But naw, you just had to play mista love a man, you had to stop and talks to that their gal. You big dummy! Man, I should punch—

DI: Hold on, PJ. I's still gots my nickel.

PJ: I don't knows why I still hangs out with you. I guess evens you needs a friend.

DI: Is your nose all right?

They just looked at each other and started laughing.

The Country Bumkins Get New Shoes

It was early in the morning, and PJ was at home, and before he could get out of the bed, DI climbed through the window. PJ's mom walked into the room.

PJ'S MOM: Oh, good morning, DI. I didn't see you come in.

Have you been here all night?

DI: No, mam, I's just gots here.

PJ'S MOM: Oh, you came through the window again, huh? DI, you do know that we have a front door. Now I see why my son still talks like that. Look, DI, you don't have to put a s behind all your words, and oh, never mind . . . PJ, guess what, we're going to buy you some new shoes today.

PJ: Aw . . .

DI: Man, we gonna gets us some new shoes. How I do?

PJ'S MOM: You did fine, DI, you did fine.

PJ: What you mean we going get some new shoes?

PJ'S MOM: Well, I wasn't planning on it, but I guess I can do it. Yes, DI, I'll get you a pair also.

DI: We's getting new shoes, we is getting new shoes! PJ, why you so down? We's getting new shoes! And since we is going with your mom, can't nothing happens to us.

PJ: That's what I's afraid of.

PJ'S MOM: Now, PJ, get up, so you can eat your breakfast. Uh, DI, have you had any breakfast?

DI: Naw, my mom still sleep. She ain't got up yet.

PJ'S MOM: Do you want some breakfast?

DI: I show do. Thank you!

PJ: Oh boy.

DI: PJ, man, you show do worries too much.

PJ: DI, you, my friend, and I likes you, but I beginning to thank you ain't nothing but bad luck.

DI: Now you done gone and hurts my feelings.

PJ: Man, I's don't mean to hurts your feelings. Come on, let's eat.

DI: Okay. Feelings better!

After breakfast, PJ's mom was ready to go.

PJ'S MOM: PJ, I want you and DI to at least brush your hair.

I don't know why you boys like to go around all day with a nappy head.

Just then, PJ had a thought.

PJ: Man, I ain't to sure we is going get new shoes.

DI: What you mean? You show do worries a lot for a big fella.

PJ: I's just trying to warn you.

DI: Man, come on.

PJ'S MOM: You two ready to go?

DI: We is ready.

They walked to the car, a 1960 Ford Falcon. It had a few rust spots, but that was the best that PJ's mom could do at the time. They all got into the car. She turned the key, but it wouldn't start. PJ turned and looked at DI.

DI: Man, what you look at me for? I didn't do nothing.

PJ'S MOM: I don't understand, it was running fine yesterday.

Maybe it's the battery. Boys, can you two go down the street for me to Mr. Cyrus's house and ask him if he could come look at my car for me? Oh, and tell him that I think it's the battery.

Once again, PJ looked at DI.

They left to go to Mr. Cyrus's house, which was about three blocks away. PJ thought to himself, *What could go wrong in three blocks? I'm with DI. Anything is possible!*

DI: Hey, PJ, man, look over yonder. That apple tree is just as full as that old potbellied pig.

PJ: Looks here, DI, we ain't going to go over no fence and get none of them their apples!

DI: Man, you know you want um, and stop being so scare.

PJ: Man, all we gots to do is to go to Mr. Cyrus's house and tells him what Momma said!

DI: Look, it ain't going take but a second.

PJ: Okay, but if—

DI: Come on, man!

But just as soon as they made it to the tree, this big kid came from around it.

BIG KID: What yall doing, trying to steal my apples?

DI: Naw, man, we just taking a shortcut.

PJ just turned his head, but as he was about to walk away, he felt hands on both of his arms. He was spun around, and then he was punched in the nose. He thought, *Not again.*

But this time PJ decided to fight back. He knocked the big kid on the ground. The kid got up and ran into the house.

DI: My man! I knows you could do it.

PJ: Let's go, man!

DI: He ain't coming back. We can gets some of these apples.

But then all of a sudden, the big kid with two other big kids started running toward them. PJ grabbed DI by the arm and pulled him across the field and then threw him over the fence. And they ran all the way to Mr. Cyrus's house. When they made it, PJ looked at DI, he would have hit him, but he was his best friend. They knocked on the door, but there was no answer, so PJ called his name.

PJ: Mr. Cyrus, is you in there?

DI: Yeah, Mr. Cyrus, is you in there?

PJ: If he's in there, I think he would have heard me.

YOUNG GIRL: Oh hello. You looking for my daddy?

DI: Oh hi!

YOUNG GIRL: Oh, DI, you pretending not to know me now?

DI: Oh hi, Pebbles.

PJ: Hi, Pebbles? Man, you—

PEBBLES: You looking for my daddy, or, DI, did you come to see me?

DI: Your daddy!

PJ turned and looked at DI.

PJ: Pebbles, huh?

Just then, Mr. Cyrus walked up.

MR. CYRUS: Pebbles gal, get your fast tail in that house.

PEBBLES: Bye, DI and friend.

MR. CYRUS: What you boys need?

PJ: Mr. Cyrus, my momma car won't start, and she asked for us to ask

MR. CYRUS: I done told that there gal that she needs a battery.

You boys jump on the back of the truck. Come on, let go!

Just then, Pebbles ran out of the screen door.

PEBBLES: Bye, DI.

DI just dropped his head.

PJ: Naw, what you dropping your head for? You and Pebbles got something going on? Pebbles and DI sitting in the tree, K-I-S-S-I-N-G.

DI: Naw, man, she just got a crush on me. She young.

They made it to PJ's house.

MR. CYRUS: Hey, Ms. Bertha.

MS. BERTHA: Hey, Mr. Cyrus.

DI: Man, Mr. Cyrus is sweet on your momma!

PJ: Man, you must be crazy. He too old.

DI: I thank your momma like him too.

PJ punched DI in the arm.

DI: Man, that hurt!

PJ: Shut your mouth then!

Mr. Cyrus got the car started.

MS. BERTHA: Thank you, Mr. Cyrus. How much I owe you?

MR. CYRUS: Now, Ms. Bertha, you know you don't owe me a thang. But like I done told you, you be needing a new battery.

MS. BERTHA: I guess I'll go ahead and get one. Thanks again.

They got into the car, and Ms. Bertha drove them to the barbershop.

DI: This ain't no shoe shop!

PJ: Man, I done told you that I didn't wants to go no way. Momma, what you 'bout to do?

MS. BERTHA. I saw that you boys needed haircuts, so I've decided to get you two haircuts instead, and besides, the summer is just about over, and school will be starting soon.

DI: My momma done told me that.

MS. BERTHA: DI, I called your mother, and she said that she would love for me to get your hair cut.

PJ just looked at DI.

PJ. DI, man, you ain't nothing but bad luck, but you still my buddy.

The Country Bumkins' End of Summer

DI: What you so down in the face about?

PJ: You know today is our last day of freedom. We are back in school tomorrow.

DI: I's know that, so we need to enjoy every hour.

PJ: You know I think this year we are going to do things different. I'm going to pay attention and go to my classes. I'm going to be smart. I'm tired of pretending to be dumb so they can just pass us along. DI, man, from this day on, we are going to listen to my mom, and we're going to go to class and pay attention.

DI: Boy, what done got into you? Is you growing up on me?

PJ: DI, stop playing dumb. I know you can learn just like I can, so come on, man! Look, I've been with you this whole summer.

I've had two bloody noses, maybe three black eyes because of you, so if you're my friend, and we do continue to hang out, you will at least try to do something that I ask you to do.

DI: All right, man, I will give it a shot, but what if I really do need some help?

PJ: I'll tell you what, the subjects that you're strong in, you'll help me, and the subjects that I'm strong in, I'll help you, deal?

DI: Deal, but you're going to be mighty busy helping me.

PJ: DI, you're a lot smarter than you give yourself credit for.

Think about all the things we did this summer. It was you figuring out ways to get them done.

DI: Yeah, but that was street smarts.

PJ: Man, just apply your street smarts to the books, and you will figure out that all this stuff ties together.

DI: Where you getting all this stuff from? You sound like your mom's.

Just then, Pebbles walked by.

PEBBLES. Hey, DI. Hey, PJ. What are you two doing just sitting there? You do know that this is the last day of summer break and schools starts tomorrow.

DI: Yes, we know, and we are looking forward to attending school this year.

Pebble, with her mouth wide opened, just stood there.

PEBBLES: Who? What? When? How? Who done taught you to talk?

Pebbles, still in shock, started walking away backward.

PJ: DI, I told you, man, I told you that you could do it. Now all we have to do is—

DI: I know, is to apply ourselves. Man, I don't know if I want to do that. I kind of enjoy being the class clown. I get a lot of attention.

PJ: Yeah, but, man, that kind of attention, do you really want it?

True enough, they laugh in your face, but what are they saying behind your back? And besides, you're my best friend, and I want you to at least try, so how about it, buddy?

DI: Well, I'll give it a shot, but if—

PJ: Man, don't worry about it, I got you! Now come on, let's enjoy this last day of freedom! Hey, let's go in and talk to my mom, and we'll try it out on her.

DI: Try what out?

PJ: Being intelligent, knucklehead!

DI: Oh, all right.

They walked in the house, and PJ's mom was making lunch.

DI: Good afternoon, Ms. Bertha. How are you today?

MS. BERTHA: I'm fin—wait a minute. Who is this speaking? I know this isn't DI! What have gotten into you? Okay, what have you two done? What have you two gotten into? Where is DI?

PJ looked over at DI and winked his eye. They both answered at the same time.

PJ and DI: We haven't gotten into anything.

MS. BERTHA: Is it snowing out there? I can't believe my ears.

My boys are finally growing up!

DI: I guess we are.

DI and PJ sat down and ate lunch, and PJ's mom couldn't stop looking at how the two young boys were quickly becoming two young men.

We all should be so fortunate to have that one friend,
One that will stick with you through thick and thin.

Fading Faith

This is a story about a woman. Oh, let's just call her Alice, but she could very well be named Barbara, Candice, or Kim. Alice was about to lose all hope and faith in man and mankind.

You see, Alice was a nurse, and she worked in delivery. She had just started and had taken part in three deliveries, and in each case, the father of the newborn wasn't present. So with each birth, she became more and more bitter. She became so upset that she wanted to leave her job. She could not believe that a man could do this to a woman and not want to see his own child born. She even started to look at the male doctors differently. She was so bitter.

But something happened to Alice that night, something that would change her life forever.

After her shift and her third delivery, she went home more disgusted than ever.

ALICE: There are not any good men out there who are willing to step up and take care of their responsibilities. All they want to do is to lay with you, and when they get you pregnant, they run away. Lord, what are we to do?

Alice went to sleep, and it was then that she was waken up in the spirit. She was shown her last three deliveries and the circumstances behind each one of them.

VOICE: Alice, I feel your hurt, I feel your pain, and I know your heart. And now I want to show you something. Come with me.

Alice was taken up in the spirit.

VOICE: On the first delivery, her name Susan. Well, Susan was rushed to the hospital by her sister. Alice, you were looking for the father, but he wasn't there. No, he wasn't because he was a high school dropout, and he wanted a job where he could really take care of his family, so he took a job working overseas. He knew he had to do this, but he wanted to be there so bad. He's a good man.

Alice just stood there; she didn't say a word.

VOICE: Now let me tell you about the second one, Sarah. She's a different case. Sarah drove herself to the hospital. She's very independent. She's so independent that she feels like she doesn't need a man. In fact, she feels like she doesn't need anyone. The father has begged to be in her and their child's life. He has even asked her to marry him. But Sarah has insisted that she has no feelings for him, but the truth is she's been hurt, and she is so afraid to let go again. She says all she wants to do is to be alone with her child, but I see and feel her pain. So you see, once again, the father is a good man. In fact, he would continue to pursue Sarah, and they will later get married and have a beautiful family.

Alice still just stood there, but by this time, she had tears forming in her eyes.

VOICE: Now, Alice, we come to Jill. What you saw was Jill being rushed to the hospital in an ambulance and her calling out her husband's name, but once again, he wasn't there. Alice, once again, you felt her pain. You felt her loneliness. Yes, she was hurting from the labor, but even more, she had just received the news that her husband, who was a patrolman, was just shot and killed. He was working overtime because he knew that they needed the extra money. He had so much love for his wife and their child-to-be.

By this time, Alice was holding her face and sobbing.

ALICE: I had all three cases, and in all three cases, I judged and judged incorrectly, and I should know better. Am I a bad nurse?

Am I a bad person?

VOICE: No, Alice, you're not a bad nurse nor are you a bad person. You're a caring person, but you must learn not to judge things from appearance but to treat each situation for what it is.

Alice's faith in men and mankind was restored.

VOICE: Sometimes we can lose hope in our own by what we think we see on the surface, and then we can be easily influenced into so many different things.

All Alice had to do was to be willing to listen to her own heart, her inner voice.

Alice soon found herself waking up in her bed. She had a new outlook on life and a cheerful song in her heart.

You can look at others as if they were your sisters or brothers.
But one thing to remember: You should
never judge books by their covers.

Trusting Soul

Leroy and Monica were new to the area. They had only lived there for about a year or so. They began to kind of like the area, but Leroy was always suspicious, never letting his guard down. But one evening Monica convinced Leroy to go on a double date with Jim and Jane. They were from this area, and they had befriended Monica.

MONICA: Leroy, I'm telling you that these are good people.

LEROY: What make you think that these are good people? I'm not saying that they're not good, but are they good for us?

MONICA: Leroy, you're so suspicious. Your background has you where you don't trust anyone. They're only asking us to go out to dinner with them.

LEROY: So they want us to ride with them?

MONICA: Leroy, now what's wrong with that? You think they're going to kidnap us?

Leroy didn't say another word, he just stared at her, but he finally agreed to go.

All week long, he was trying to think of excuses to get out of going.

MONICA: Leroy, stop it. All week long, you have been looking for excuses, trying to find a way to get out of going. It's going to be fun, you'll see.

Finally, Friday came, and they were ready.

LEROY: Are you sure that you want to ride with them? I'll tell you one thing if we're going to ride with them, I'm going to take my old trusty knife.

MONICA: Your knife, and what's it going to do?

LEROY: You'll see. If we have to use it, you'll see. I mean, something in my bones is just not feeling right about those two.

It's like they're too friendly. I bet when they come in, they will talk about the weather. That is always a bad sign when someone comes in and start talking about the weather. It means that it's something else on their mind, but they're trying not to let it show.

MONICA: Oh, stop it. Well, they're out there now, so please be on your best behavior.

They rang the doorbell. Monica looked at Leroy.

LEROY: What?

MONICA: Are you going to answer the door?

LEROY: They're your friends, you can answer it, and besides, you might not like the way I answer it.

Monica answered the door.

MONICA: Jim, Jane, come on in. How are you two?

JIM: Howdy, well, we are just fine. Howdy, Leroy, man, I thought we were going to get some bad weather.

Leroy looked at Monica.

LEROY: Oh, you did, huh? Whatever gave you that thought?

I've listened to the weather report all week, and not one time did they say any bad weather was coming.

Jane quickly interrupted in.

JANE. My, what a lovely home you have. Those pictures, are they your children?

LEROY, whispering underneath his breath: No, they're your children.

JANE: Excuse me, Leroy, did you say something?

MONICA: No, I think he was just clearing his throat.

Weren't you, Leroy?

LEROY: So, Jim and Jane, man, it sure is funny how you two just happened to meet and have names like Jim and Jane. Just how did you two meet?

Jane looked at Jim.

JANE: Well, it's a long story. We will have to tell it to you sometime. My, look at the time. We really need to be going.

LEROY: Uh, do we have reservations or something?

JANE: Oh yes, we have reservations!

JIM: Yeah, nothing but the best for our friends! We going to eat steak and potatoes. Yeah, boy!

Monica, looked over at Leroy as if she was hoping that he wouldn't say anything.

MONICA: Well, we should be going.

As they walked toward their vehicle . . .

LEROY: Maybe we should just take our vehicle and follow you two.

JIM and JANE: No!

JANE: No, I mean, that there is no need for you all to burn your gas. We can just burn ours.

Leroy looked over at Monica as if he wanted to say something, but Monica looked at Leroy and squinted as if to tell him to keep his mouth shut.

They made it to the car, and Jim opened the door for Monica, and Leroy reluctantly opened the door for Jane.

LEROY: So tell me where are we going? I want to phone my son to let him know.

JIM: Leroy, my man, do you like steak? I like me a fat juicy steak.

I like it kind or rare. I like for it to say moo when I bite into it.

Jim and Jane started laughing.

Once again, Leroy looked over at Monica, but this time she was looking back at him. They had noticed how Jim and Jane had avoided answering their question, not saying where they were going.

JIM: Man, I tell you that I was watching this ballgame the other day, and I tell you what these white ball players ain't got a chance against them black boys. They can really play.

Leroy and Monica once again looked at each other.

After driving several backroads, they finally reached their destination. Leroy and Monica tried to get out of their back seats, but they noticed that the child-safety locks were engaged.

Jane saw that they tried to open their doors.

JANE: You know, we have to engage our child-safety locks because of our grandchildren. We often keep them, you know, we have to protect the little ones.

LEROY: Well, you don't have the little ones now.

JANE: Jim, I thought I told you to disengage those things.

JIM: Well, I'll take care of it, I'll take care of it. Let's get on in here so we can get our table.

Leroy noticed that they never disengaged the safety locks.

Leroy and Monica tried to walk slowly behind them, but they slowed down and walked beside them. When they entered, it was like all eyes were on them. Everyone was very friendly; you can say that they were overly friendly.

SUE: 'Ello, Jane, so this is them. You say, Leroy and Monica? My, they look healthy. Look like fine racehorses, fine racehorses.

JANE: Sue, why don't you just get someone to show us to our table? You all have to forgive Sue. I think she's been here for a while and has had too many drinks.

LEROY: Yeah, too many drinks. I've heard that when a person is drunk, they often say or do the things that they wanted to say or do when they were sober.

JANE: Leroy, you say some of the funniest things.

LEROY: Yeah, funny.

They finally got seated, and they ordered. Jim ordered a 14-ounce porterhouse rare, large baked potato, some mac and cheese, and a plate of buttered cornbread.

JANE: Now, Jim, are you trying to show out in front of our company?

JIM: Naw, I just feel extra good to night. I feel like I could eat the whole cow.

LEROY: Really, why are you feeling so good?

JANE: I guess it's because we're out with you two wonderful people.

JIM: Yeah, it feels like we have hit the jackpot.

Leroy looked at Monica.

LEROY: We need to go!

JANE: What, you need to go? Well, the restrooms are in the back.

MONICA: That's funny, I thought I saw a sign pointing to the restrooms up front on the other side of the room. Leroy, I think you're right, we do need to go.

JANE: Oh, those restrooms are for the employees and are probably not too clean.

MONICA: Employees, huh. I've never heard of employees' restrooms being located in the front of a restaurant.

JANE: Now, Monica, you know that we are in the country and that they do things a little different here.

At that moment, Jim received a phone call.

JIM: Jim here. Oh yeah, we are just fine, we are just fine . . . Yeah, I know what time it is. We'll be leaving here shortly . . . My wife, oh, she's right here . . . Hey, do you remember that horse?

JANE: Jim, you're being rude.

JIM: Hey, I need to go. I was just informed that I was being rude.

LEROY: Look, we appreciate you two inviting us to dinner and everything, but I think that we'll just call for a taxi or something to take us home. You two can just stay and finish enjoying yourself, and besides, it seems like you two have more plans.

JANE: Now come on, Leroy, we never think of you two having to take a taxi home. Now what type of host would we be? Maybe you just need a glass of wine or something to help you relax?

LEROY: No, I don't need a glass of wine. I need—

MONICA: Uh, Leroy, honey, maybe you do need to calm down a bit. Jane and Jim did invite us out, and they have paid for our dinner. Jane, I think Leroy is just a bit tired, and maybe we do need to be going.

JANE: Well, maybe you're right. Jim, why don't you go use the restroom before we go?

Jim got up from the table, but not thinking, he walked into the front restroom, and when he entered, he was joined by three other guys.

Leroy, not one to not pay attention to his surroundings, asked Jane a question.

LEROY: Jane, I thought you said that the front set of restrooms were for the employees?

JANE: Oh, Leroy, we come here so often that they just let us use them.

LEROY: I guess those three other fellows come here just as much?

MONICA, whispering: Leroy, calm down, sweetie. We're about to leave.

Jim exited the restroom with a huge catlike smile on his face.

JIM: Jane, honey, it looks like our horses are going to pay off!

Jane looked at Jim out of the corner of her eyes.

JANE: Now, Jim, let's not bore Leroy and Monica talking about our horses.

JIM: Yeah, maybe you're right. You two fillies ready to go?

Jane elbowed Jim.

As Leroy stood up, he patted his pocket. He wanted to make sure that he still had his utility knife in there.

JIM: Come on, you two, we going to have us a good time.

LEROY: Oh, you two do have plans after you drop us off?

JANE: I think what Jim meant was we have had a good time just being out with you all.

Leroy looked at Monica, and this time Monica had a look of concern on her face.

They left the restaurant and made it to their car. As they got in, Leroy tried to disengage the child-safety lock, but it had been filed off.

They reluctantly got in.

As they drove off, Leroy noticed that they were taking a different way.

LEROY: Hey, aren't you going the wrong way?

JANE: Well, we thought we would go a different way and show you two some of the scenery around here.

LEROY: But it's pitch-black. What scenery is there for us to see, and why are you taking all these back roads? I think you just need to pull over right now. We'll walk home!

JIM: Boy! You just need to sit back and shut your mouth. I'm tired of all the noise you done been keeping up all night!

Leroy looked at Monica. She had tears flowing down her cheeks.

He then took out his knife and used the glass-break end, broke the side window, punched the window out, unlocked the door, reached out, and opened it. He grabbed Monica by the hand. Jim, not thinking, jammed his brakes, and they jumped out of the vehicle and started running the other way.

Jim and Jane jumped out of the vehicle and looked.

JANE: Jim, you and your big mouth! Get back in the car!

JIM: Well, you know all they're going to do is call the police, and when they do, we'll be waiting for them.

Leroy and Monica ran in the opposite direction just until they got out of sight. Then they ducked into the woods. Monica pulled out her phone.

LEROY: Who are you calling?

MONICA: The police!

LEROY: Don't! Wait!

MONICA: What do you mean?

LEROY: Didn't you see the sticker on their car? It said that they support the police. I just want to see if the police support them.

MONICA: Oh, I see.

LEROY: Look! The police. I want you to remember the number on that police car, 54.

MONICA: Why do you want me to remember the number?

LEROY: Well, you see, that car is assigned to an officer. I can find out who it is. Be quiet. I want to hear what they're talking about.

JIM: I told you that they were some thoroughbreds. You should have seen them run.

OFFICER 54: Look, we need to find them. I bet we can have a lot of fun with them two, and from what you two told me about the female, I just might want to jump in the saddle and ride. If she's any good, I just might keep her around a little while before I dispatch her. Hell, that other old gal, she was a fighter, and she sure knew how to bulk. I kind of hate that she got pregnant, and I had to kill her.

POLICE DISPATCHER: Car 54.

OFFICER 54: Uh, go ahead for car 54.

POLICE DISPATCHER: Car 54, we have a 911 hang-up in the area of horse stable road and railroad.

OFFICER 54: Ten-four.

Leroy turned and looked at Monica.

MONICA: I'm sorry I had dialed 911, but I hung up when you told me not to call.

LEROY: Never mind, I think we've heard. Wait a minute.

OFFICER 54: Car 54, 10-97 in the area. I think my captain is getting somewhat suspicious of me. So I need to not find these two, but what I can do is to wait until it's all finished and get a tip from two reliable witnesses that just happen to be on a walk and find two bodies.

Of course, this is after we're all finished with them.

The three of them started laughing.

Leroy had heard all that he needed to hear. Leroy pulled out his cell phone and called the captain.

CAPTAIN: Leroy, you got something for me?

LEROY: Yes, I have your officer and two other citizens, but I don't think this will be all of them, but since I have my wife with me, I'm not going to push it any further. We're at horse stable road and railroad.

CAPTAIN: Your wife?

LEROY: Yeah, you said that they were taking couples, so this was the only way that I was able. Hell, just call in the cavalry!

CAPTAIN: They're on their way. They should be there in two.

OFFICER 54: I see others coming. We need to play it cool.

Let's pretend that I just made it here, you know, the same routine.

That officer was in for a surprise.

OFFICER 54: Captain? I didn't know you were working the streets tonight. Well, we have these two here, and they said that they saw two people.

CAPTAIN: Cut it! You're under arrest, you and your accomplices.

At that time, Leroy and his wife walked out from the woods. He was holding a recorder in his hand, and a special agent badge was on his chest.

CAPTAIN: Great work, Leroy, as usual.

Monica looked at Leroy.

CAPTAIN: I think you just might have some explaining to do.

LEROY: Yeah, I see. I rather talk to you, but I know that I can't avoid it any longer.

Monica was just standing there, looking at Leroy like she wanted to cut his throat.

LEROY: Monica, sweetheart, I—

MONICA: Why didn't you tell me? You used me as bait.

LEROY: No, honey, this wasn't how it was supposed to go down, but you kept insisting that we go out with them. They had been on our radar for a string of missing and murdered people. Baby, I never wanted you to be in harm's way. I'm truly sorry.

MONICA: No, I meant, why didn't you tell me that you were still working?

They looked at each other, and they laughed, hugged, and kissed.

LEROY: I love you!

In every profession, there's good and bad.
You can't judge them all by the experience
someone else might have had.

A Mother's Love

This is a story about a young boy named John and his mother.

MOMMA: John, it's time to get up. I know it's the summer and you don't have school, but you're not going to stay in bed all day.

JOHN: But, Momma, it's only eight o'clock.

MOMMA: Uh, I'm not going to say it again. I've cooked breakfast, it's on the table, so get up and brush your teeth and wash your face so we can sit down and eat.

John was a usual ten-year-old, and he didn't understand why his mother wanted him to get up so early and eat breakfast with her, but he slowly got up and went into the bathroom and did his morning rituals. After he finished, he went in and sat at the table.

JOHN: Momma, I don't understand it. David gets to get up when he wants to. After all, it is summer, and we don't have school.

MOMMA: Well, John, David is not my child, and he is not my responsibility. Now bless the food so we can eat. And besides, I want you to learn that you can't sleep all day and expect to get things accomplished.

John blessed the food, and he also blessed his mother.

MOMMA: That was sweet, John. Thank you for thinking about me this morning.

Underneath John's breath, he was asking the Lord to bless his mom and bless him by letting him sleep longer.

MOMMA: Now when you're finished, I want you to hurry up and change your bed linen. I've already set out some clean linen for you.

JOHN: But, Mom, it's only been about three weeks since I changed them the last time.

MOMMA: Three weeks for you is more like three months. And after you've done that, I want you to sweep and mop your floor. That also means that you pick up everything off your floor first. Oh, and make sure you put your dirty clothes into the clothes basket. No clothes stuck together! The white clothes with the whites, and the color clothes with the colors.

JOHN, whispering underneath his breath: Yes, um, boss, I work like a slave.

MOMMA: And no, you're not a slave, you're my son, and I love you very much. This will pay off in the long run, you will see.

JOHN: When?

MOMMA: Well, one day you will have responsibilities, and if you're able to handle these little things, you'll be able to take care of greater things.

John didn't understand what the heck his mother was talking about. All he knew was that he was having to clean his room, and for what? He knew that it was going to get dirty all over again.

Time went by.

MOMMA: John, are you finished with those things?

JOHN: Yes, I'm finished.

MOMMA: Well, come on, son. You know that I have to go to work.

JOHN: Mom, why do I have to go over to Aunt Paula's house?

She always wants to kiss me on my cheek, and then she makes me clean her fence and chop around her sidewalk.

MOMMA: A little work never hurts anyone, and besides, you know that I can't leave you here all alone.

JOHN: Why not? You keep saying that I'm growing up fast.

MOMMA: Yeah, but not that fast!

Johnny and his mother soon left for her sister's house.

MOMMA: John, you behave yourself and do what your aunt Paula says. I love you.

JOHN: I love you too.

AUNT PAULA: All right, girl, don't you worry about little Johnny. You know that he is well taken care of . . . Now give your auntie a little kiss.

John reluctantly let his aunt give him a kiss on his cheek, but as he walked away, he wiped it off.

AUNT PAULA: Johnny, I got my hoe sharpened, so it won't be as hard on you this time. I like for you to chop around my fence and pull those old vines off for me.

JOHN: Aunt Paula.

AUNT PAULA: Yes, Johnny!

JOHN: Never mind. Can I use your bathroom first and wait for some more of the morning dew to burn off?

AUNT PAULA: Yeah, Johnny. While we wait, you can help me shell these peas. I have three bushels.

Johnny just held his head down and went into the bathroom.

And when he came out, his aunt handed him a bowl, purple hull peas, and a brown paper bag. He sat down beside her, and they started shelling peas. He shelled until his finger were sore and turning purple.

JOHN: Aunt Paula, can I go out and get started in the yard now?

Aunt Paula laughed.

AUNT PAULA: Yes, you can go out and get started, and I will have you some lunch ready in a few hours.

Well, a few years went by, and John was now thirteen. He would now get up, get his bed made, straighten up his room, and start breakfast all before eight o'clock.

His mother shouted from her bedroom.

MOMMA: Johnny, what are you doing? Uh, you do realize that today is Saturday.

JOHN: Mom, I know what today is. I just thought I would get up and cook you breakfast, and besides, I wanted to ask you something.

MOMMA: Oh, I see. Are you trying to butter me up for something?

JOHN: No, Mom, I really just wanted to do this for you, but I wanted to ask you if you would be open to us getting a dog.

MOMMA: A dog! Johnny, a dog, well, let me think about it.

What Johnny didn't know was that his mother was already planning on getting him a boxer. She knew that's what he wanted.

Several times she saw him looking at them online. The puppies were already born, she had already placed a deposit on one, and now all she had to do was to wait about another week before she could pick him up.

MOMMA: Johnny, are you sure you're ready for a dog? You do know that they're a big responsibility.

JOHN: Mom, you've been preparing me my whole life to be responsible, and now when it's time for me to show you—

MOMMA: Well, like I said, we'll see.

The week soon passed, and his mother picked up the puppy and took it home.

MOMMA: John, where are you? I have a surprise for you.

John came out of his room and saw the puppy walking around in the living room.

JOHN: No, you didn't. No, you didn't! Mom, you got me a puppy, a boxer puppy at that! I can tell! Look at his round head, and his tail is already cut, Mom!

MOMMA: I take it that you approve. Now let me lay down the rules. First, this is your puppy and not mine. Second, you will be responsible for his house training. You will be responsible for feeding him and getting up and taking him out, and we will take him to the vet and groomers together.

JOHN: Okay, Mom, I know exactly how to train him. Hey, what about a name?

MOMMA: Well, he is your puppy. You can name him.

JOHN: Okay. I'll call him Popeye. Yeah, that's it—Popeye.

MOMMA: Popeye? Why Popeye?

JOHN: Look at his eyes. One looks bigger than the other.

They both laughed.

It didn't take long; the puppy grew, and John was now a senior in high school. He, his mother, and Popeye lived and were very happy.

MOMMA: John, you only have a week left in high school, and then what? Are you still set on joining the military? What about Popeye?

JOHN: Momma, you know that Popeye is more your dog than mine. From the first day, you haven't let me do anything for him. All you let me do was to name him, and you questioned that.

MOMMA: John, I just wanted to make sure that the military is what you really wanted. Son, I want you to know that I'm happy for you and that I love you very much. And for Popeye, well, I knew that you would be leaving someday, so I just wanted to get a head start on taking care of him.

They both laughed.

JOHN: Momma, I want to thank you for raising me up to be respectful and to be responsible. Mom, I would not be in this position now if it had not been for you. Oh yeah, and Auntie Paula also.

They both laughed again.

The love that you get from your mother
is greater than what you might get from another.
There's only one greater love,
and that is the love that you get from above.

One Dark Night

One dark and lonely night, while I was lying in my bed, I decided to get up and go lie on my couch instead. While laying on my couch, my eyes started to get heavy, and they started to blink, and then my mind started to wonder, and I started to think.

But all of a sudden, I heard this sound. It was like some large footsteps hitting the ground.

I thought surely no one came in through my door, but I still heard the footsteps walking across my floor.

If I was in my bed, this would be the time with my covers. I would have covered my head.

The footsteps seemed to get closer, and then they stopped in front of me. For some odd reason, I was too afraid to open my eyes and see.

I began to open my mouth, and I started to pray, but there were no words. I didn't know what to say.

I finally opened my eyes, and what did I see? There was no one there, no one besides me.

So I settled back down and thought this must have been a dream, but then I felt a hand in my back. I wanted to scream.

All of a sudden, a deep chill came over me. I thought again, *Who or what could this be?*

The next morning, when I thought that I had awaken, I felt no pain. I felt no cold. I didn't even feel like I was old.

I wasn't even hungry. I didn't want anything to eat. I felt as if I was still asleep.

I thought to myself that I would get on with my day, but for some reason, I felt like at home is where I wanted to stay.

In my heart, I knew that something was wrong, but yet I still stood there, trying to be strong.

The day would go by, and it didn't matter how hard I tried.

I couldn't force a tear from my eye.

No one called, no one said anything at all.

My sense of reality seemed to fade. I didn't even feel the sun nor did I feel the shade.

I wanted to be heard, I wanted to shout with my voice, but it felt like I couldn't, and I didn't have a choice. In my heart, I felt like giving him praise, so with my voice and my hands, I tried raise.

Then all of a sudden, the morning sun would hit my face, the thought of the night before was gone, and there was no sign nor was there any trace.

But I knew in my heart that something was new. It was like I was able to see right from wrong. I knew what was true.

The visitor that I had had changed me, but for what reason, I guess I have to wait and see.

What's so funny is that he didn't say a word, but in my heart, his voice, I still heard.

He didn't have to say much, but he did all this with one simple little touch.

The unspoken word is enough to be heard.

A Letter to My Friend

I pray, as you receive this letter, it finds you in great health and sound mind. In case you didn't know, I've done it. I won the lottery. Well, I guess I've won. You know what they say, you can gain the world, but to lose your soul, huh?

Yeah, I no longer live in that small town. I guess you can say that I've moved on up, or have I? I think back of the people I left behind. No, I wouldn't call most friends, just people. And then again, I think, have I lived or have I just begun to live?

I know that this letter might be confusing. Well, to be completely honest, it's somewhat confusing to me. As I write, I often have to stop and wipe the tears from my eyes. Yet I have to continue reminding myself "that I'm the righteous of God in Christ Jesus."

I guess I find myself doing it quite often. You see, whenever a negative thought comes into my head, I have to remind myself "that I am the righteous of God in Christ Jesus." A negative thought, yeah, I know what you're thinking. You're thinking, why should I be thinking negative thoughts, or why should I want to commit suicide?

Well, there is more than one negative thought, and I never said anything about suicide. I'm going to ask you a question: Have you ever thought about just leaving and giving it all up? I mean, your life as you now have. No, I'm not talking about going into the woods and becoming a hermit, you know, just like starting over. I wonder, can you truly start over?

Oh, the negative thoughts? Thoughts, like I was saying, just giving all of it up, just walking away from everyone, family, friends, job, and those associates. I know what you're saying. I've won this money, and now I've lost my mind. No. What if I just now found my mind? Or you might be thinking now that I have money, I want to get away from everyone so that I won't have to share. Well, do I have to share? No!

No, I don't have to share, and I learned that also. If you share with others, it's never enough, so it's probably better not sharing at all. The people who are going to be in your life are going to be there, and the ones who are not, well, they're not. So is that thought negative, or is it just a sane thought? I guess it depends on the way you look at it.

Do you ever feel like you're all alone in this world? I mean, you can be surrounded by people and family, yet you still feel like you're all alone. You feel like God has left you to face your thoughts and demons all by yourself. You know, I was feeling like this, and then a poem came in my head, and as I wrote the poem, it didn't seem to speak to me, but as I went back and read over it again, it was speaking directly to me. Well, I guess I'll write it down for you.

You know what they say, when the Lord wants you to speak to someone else, he speaks to you first or something like that. Anyway, here it is. It's called "Standing Alone":

As I walk through the valley of shadows of death,
As I pass by a mirror, I stopped and took a good look at myself
I felt as if I was all alone
Right then and there, I wanted to go home
I heard a voice coming from deep inside
I wanted to run, I wanted to hide
I looked around, and as far as I could see,
There was no one else there besides me
The voice told me not to be afraid or not to fear
Because if I knew who it was, I would be full of cheer
I asked, through all my hard times, why have you forsaken me?
Because it was during those times I was by myself as far as I could see
He didn't say another word. He just let me talk
I wanted to leave, I wanted to run, but I couldn't even walk
And then I took a look back over my years
I looked at the times that I had shed many tears
I looked at the times that I've done things that I shouldn't have done
All because they made me feel good and I thought that they were fun
All the times that I thought that I couldn't make it
All the times that I wanted to just give up and quit
And then I thought and I fell down on my knee
It was you. You, Lord, you were the one that saved me
I thought to myself your love and your grace, I do not deserve
But yet it's me that you continue to serve
I ask, why do you do so much for me?
Is there something in me that I don't see?

He told me to get up and go
He said that when the time is right, then you will know
I was able to open my eyes and stand up
I no longer felt like I was stuck
As I started to dry my eyes and walk away
He said, "All I ask you to do is continue to pray."
And from that very day and on
I knew that I would never have to stand alone

Now you can see how this poem might have spoken to me.

This poem is one of the reasons that I constantly remind myself that I'm the righteous of God in Christ Jesus. I guess, if I am to believe it, I want to hear it as often as I can. And why not?

We are constantly fed the negative thoughts and events of this world, so why not feed yourself some positive thoughts as often as possible? Every day, when you turn on the TV, the Internet, and now even your cell phones, you see or hear some negativity. It's enough to make you wish that you were never born.

Speaking of never being born, can you truly imagine what might have been if you weren't ever born. Just think about the people's lives that you've touched besides mine. I know it's kind of hard to remember every small thing you might have done in your life, but just think about it, from maybe a conversation, a smile, or just your presence, and not to mention any physical thing that you might have done, the impact that you might have made. Just think about if you weren't here.

Well, I guess I'll end this letter. I know your eyes are getting tired. So until next time, my friend. Love you.

Some might point the finger of blame.
Who is crazy, or who is sane?
Can you tell who is happy or who is sad,
or who is angry or who is mad?
Words can play an important part.
But are the words the ending, or are they the start?

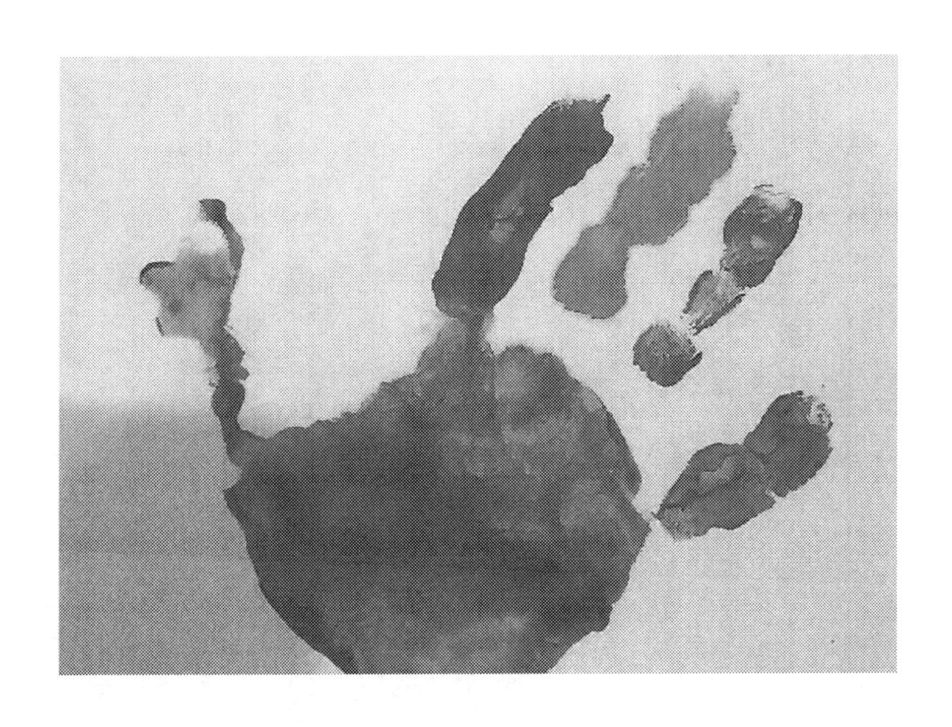

Photo by Ryle's Photography

Your author Paul Jones was born in Pine Bluff, Arkansas. Although born and raised in the South, his experiences have taken him as far as California, Germany, and Honduras, to name a few. He has over fourteen years in the United States Armed Forces, as well as twenty-three years in law enforcement. As a law enforcement officer, he has served as a member of SWAT, bike patrol and school resource, and a director of security for a local high school. He is a member of Alpha Phi Alpha Fraternity Inc. Delta Sigma Lambda chapter.

He has a bachelor's degree in criminal justice from American Intercontinental University, where he graduated summa cum laude. He has other books to his credit: *Waking Up*, *Life and Love and Living Life Poems to Live By*. Paul has also received many awards.

Printed in the United States
by Baker & Taylor Publisher Services